DUTCH SNEAKERS AND FLEA-KEEPERS

14 MORE STORIES

BY CALEF BROWN

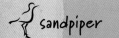 sandpiper

Houghton Mifflin Harcourt
Boston   New York

for Phebe

www.sandpiperbooks.com

Art Direction/Design: George Mimnaugh

The text of this book is set in Emigre™, Mrs. Eaves Roman.

Library of Congress Cataloging-in-Publication Data
Brown, Calef.
Dutch sneakers and fleakeepers: 14 more stories / Calef Brown.
p.   cm.
Summary: Fourteen poems about quirky subjects and characters.
HC ISBN-13: 978-0-618-05183-0
PA ISBN-13: 978-0-547-23751-0
1. Children's poetry, American. [1. American poetry.] I. Title.
PS3552.R68525   D8   2000
811'.54—dc21   99-053722

Manufactured in Singapore
TWP 10 9 8 7 6 5

CONTENTS

DUTCH SNEAKERS

MOON REUNION

OLF

GUMBUBBLE MONDAY

TATTLESNAKE

SIR DANCE-A-LOT

LITTLE NED

THE RUNAWAY WAFFLE

FLEAKEEPERS

MYSTERIOUS FISH

SEVEN BAD TEETH

JACK IN THE BUCKET

MAGIC ELECTRIC GUITAR

SUGAR BEACH

DUTCH SNEAKERS

My Dutch Wooden Sneakers from Holland,
the grooviest shoes on the block.
I love 'em so much,
did I mention they're Dutch?
I don't care if it hurts when I walk.

My Dutch Wooden Sneakers from Holland,
handmade out of some sort of pine.
They creak and they squeak,
and they constantly leak,
but I just can't believe that they're mine!

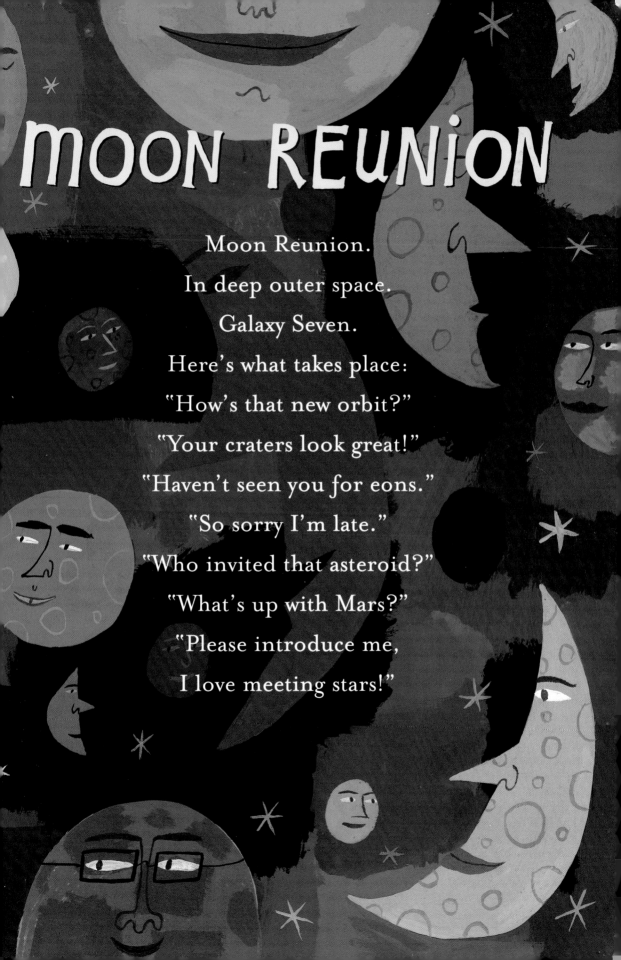

MOON REUNION

Moon Reunion.

In deep outer space.

Galaxy Seven.

Here's what takes place:

"How's that new orbit?"

"Your craters look great!"

"Haven't seen you for eons."

"So sorry I'm late."

"Who invited that asteroid?"

"What's up with Mars?"

"Please introduce me,

I love meeting stars!"

OLF

Olf is a terrible pirate,
with a rabbit instead of a parrot.
He couldn't afford
the usual sword,
so he has to get by with a carrot.

Olf makes a racket
wherever he goes.
Screaming "Shiver me fingers!"
and "Off with your nose!"

His leg has no peg,
and his beard isn't blue,
but Olf is a pirate.
I'm frightened,
aren't you?

GUMBUBBLE MONDAY

Gumbubble Monday,
this is how it goes:
Gobble up your bubble gum,
put on your finest fancy clothes.
Take the bus down Wiggly Street,
chewing all the way.
Hop out on the double,
then blow a big bubble.
You're suddenly floating away!

TATTLESNAKE

An odd little creature

that every kid fears

is a snake

with unusual stripes

and big ears.

It spies on you,

tells on you,

then disappears.

Leaving the house

with your parents in tears.

Now because of that snake,

and one small mistake,

you're in trouble

for sixty or seventy years!

SiR DANCE-A-LOT

Here we've got
Sir Dance-a-lot.
He's really quite a charmer.
With metal pants,
come watch him dance
all night in shining armor.

In days of old,
or so I'm told,
he used to run the castle.
No time for fighting dragons now,
he says, "That's such a hassle."

LiTTLE NED

Little Ned got a rash
on the back of his neck.
He wouldn't stop scratching for days.
His grandmother gave him
a jar of strange ointment.
His mom and dad said, "It's only a phase."

The doctor's solution was simple:
a plastic adjustable cone,
to keep Ned from scratching
the back of his neck.
He just couldn't leave it alone.

the RUNAWAY WAFFLE

Suzy nibbles waffle.

Waffle runs away.

Suzy chases after waffle.

Waffle likes to play.

Suzy never catches waffle.

Waffle doesn't stop.

Suzy gets all tuckered out

and drinks a bottle of pop.

FLEAKEEPERS

Calling all fleakeepers!

Make lots of cash!

Raise fleas in your basement,

just feed 'em your trash.

These cute little fellers

are eager to please.

They learn to speak German

more quickly than bees.

You can teach them to whistle

in less than a day.

Believe it or not,

many people will pay

up to ten thousand bucks

for a talented flea.

Don't know about you,

but that sounds good to me!

mysterious fish

Mysterious fish tank.
Mysterious fish.
Green like asparagus.
Flat like a dish.
Toss in a peppercorn,
then make a wish.
Mysterious fish tank.
Mysterious fish.

SEVEN BAD TEETH

Look over yonder.
Well what do you know?
Seven bad teeth in a row.
Down in the mouth,
where there's no place to go.
They already have cavities
(thirteen or so).

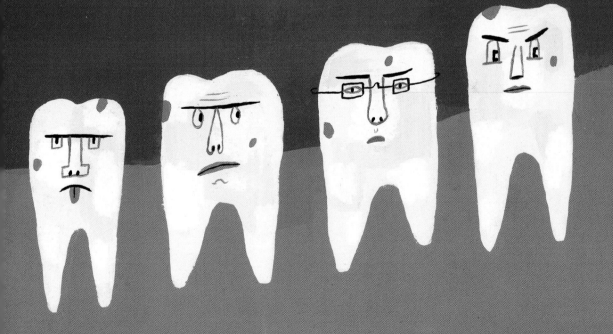

But these teeth aren't so bad,
like me and like you,
they just need a cleaning
and something to chew.

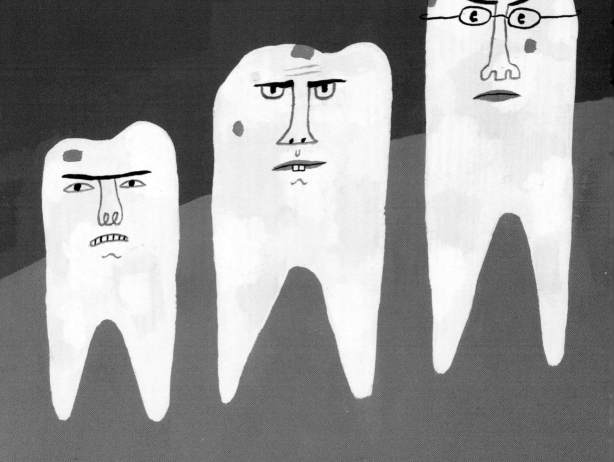

Jack in the Bucket

There once was a man from Nantucket,

not a person exactly,

a Jack in the Bucket.

A sort of a joker.

A dunce, if you will.

A doofus,

a dingus,

a regular pill.

In a pail

on the beautiful isle of Nantucket.

There once was a Jack in the Bucket.

MaGic ELECTRIC GUiTAR

Grandmother's magic electric guitar.
Nobody knew it would take her so far.
From Oslo to Glasgow,
she jams all night long.
Her fans hold their hands up
before every song.

One tune they adore
is called "Eardrum Surprise."
In the crowd
it's so loud
you get tears in your eyes.

Keep rockin',
dear Grandma,
wherever you are.
On that musical magic electric guitar.

SUGAR BEACH

Donut Beetles
very slowly
crossing Sugar Beach.
One delicious donut each.
A tasty treat
when they finally reach
the sea.